Welcome to RAINBOW FALLS!

Adapted by Olivia London

Based on the episode "Rainbow Falls" written by Corey Powell

LITTLE, BROWN & COMPANY
LB kids

"Twilight!" Spike calls, bursting through the front door of the Golden Oak Library with a scroll tightly gripped in his claw. "We got an official letter from the mayor of Ponyville!"

"Really?" Twilight Sparkle cries out, dropping the encyclopedia she is reading and rushing to greet her best friend. "Well, open it and see what it says!"

Little, Brown and Company

Hachette Book Group
1290 Avenue of the Americas, New York, NY 10104
Visit our website at lb-kids.com

LB kids is an imprint of Little, Brown and Company.
The LB kids name and logo are trademarks of Hachette Book Group, Inc.

The publisher is not responsible for websites (or their content) that are not owned by the publisher.

First Edition: April 2014

Library of Congress Control Number: 2013955548

ISBN 978-0-316-24796-2

10 9 8 7 6

CW

Printed in the United States of America

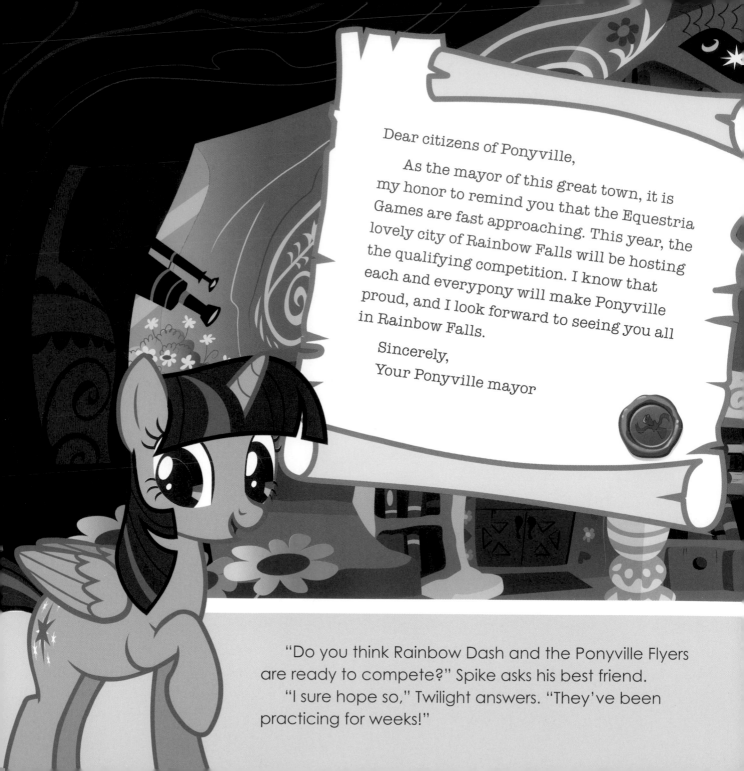

Dear citizens of Ponyville,

As the mayor of this great town, it is my honor to remind you that the Equestria Games are fast approaching. This year, the lovely city of Rainbow Falls will be hosting the qualifying competition. I know that each and everypony will make Ponyville proud, and I look forward to seeing you all in Rainbow Falls.

Sincerely,
Your Ponyville mayor

"Do you think Rainbow Dash and the Ponyville Flyers are ready to compete?" Spike asks his best friend.

"I sure hope so," Twilight answers. "They've been practicing for weeks!"

A few days later, it is time to leave for Rainbow Falls.

"Isn't this exciting, Spike?" Twilight remarks as she packs a few final things, including her travel guide. "I've never been to Rainbow Falls before! I can't wait to learn all about it."

"I wish I could come with you," Spike says longingly.

"I do, too," Twilight replies. "But Fluttershy is trusting you to watch over all her sick animal friends while we're gone, and that's a much more important responsibility."

"You're right!" Spike says. "I'm going to be the best critter-sitter ever!"

"That's the spirit!" Twilight agrees. "I promise I'll send you lots of postcards."

"Thanks, Twilight. I'll miss you!"

"Aww, I'll miss you, too, Spike!" she says, giving her friend one last hug before heading out the door. "See you in a few days!"

"All aboard the Friendship Express!" the conductor calls out over the loudspeaker. "All aboard!"

"I wonder what Rainbow Falls will be like," Fluttershy asks.

"I hear there are glorious, sparkling rainbows everywhere!" says Rarity.

"I hear the Rainbow Falls arena is enormous!" Rainbow Dash adds.

"Well, I hear they have a whole marketplace where ponies sell souvenirs and things for the games," Applejack begins. "I'm gonna set up my wagon there and sell my delicious apple brown Bettys to all the contestants."

Suddenly, everypony gasps and stares at Applejack.

"Don't worry, y'all!" she cries. "I'll make sure to save enough for you to load up on. I promise!"

The ponies let out a sigh of relief!

The friends are so busy talking that the hours fly by. Before they know it, the conductor makes an announcement.

"This station stop is Rainbow Falls! Watch your hooves while getting off the train! This stop: Rainbow Falls!"

"This is breathtaking!" Rarity remarks as she looks at hundreds of beams of light shooting down through the clouds, casting rainbows across the city.

The ponies leave the train station and head toward their hotel. On the way, they take in the beautiful rainbow scenery.

"It says here in my travel guide that Rainbow Falls was built on a cliff next to a waterfall," Twilight Sparkle tells her friends. "That's why there are always so many natural rainbows all over the town."

"Well, these Rainbow Falls ponies sure do make good use of them," Applejack says.

No more than a minute after dropping their bags in the room, Rainbow Dash announces, "Fluttershy and I are heading straight to the arena. We need to start practicing right away!"

Dear Spike,

Rainbow Falls is just as pretty as we all imagined! The ponies are so friendly, and they are very excited to be hosting the qualifying competition for the Equestria Games. Everypony left already to explore the city and start practicing for the races, but I stayed in the hotel to write to you, of course!

Our hotel is right in the center of the city. It's built into the side of a small waterfall, so the view from our room is really cool! Well, I'm off to go exploring now. I promise to write again soon!

XOXO,
Twilight Sparkle

Twilight Sparkle decides to explore the city of Rainbow Falls before joining the Ponyville Flyers in the Rainbow Falls arena, where they are practicing.

"'The Rainbow River, which runs all the way through Rainbow Falls,'" Twilight Sparkle reads aloud to herself, "'is one of the longest rivers in Equestria and—'"

Thump! With her head buried in the book, Twilight accidentally bumps into some ponies.

"Ouch!" comes a familiar squeak.

"Pinkie Pie? Rarity?" Twilight calls.

"Gee, Twilight, that really hurt," Pinkie Pie says, rubbing her head with her hoof.

"I'm sorry! I should have been paying more attention to where I was walking," Twilight apologizes. "But this book is just so fascinating!"

"Well, I think you should put the book down and explore the town using your eyes," Rarity says. "I need to go shopping for the Ponyville uniforms!"

"I'm right behind you," Twilight replies happily.

Dear Spike,

I spent the whole day walking around the center of Rainbow Falls today with Pinkie Pie and Rarity. We had a great time, but boy, am I tired! Rainbow Falls has lots of great shops and stores. The Rainbow River runs straight through the town, so there are lots of nice wooden bridges to walk across and benches to sit on by the water. They are perfect for reading my guidebook! I hope you're having fun with Fluttershy's animal friends. Miss you!

Your friend,
Twilight

The next day, Twilight Sparkle, Rarity, and Pinkie Pie get up early and head straight to the marketplace.

"Ooh, I can't wait to get some sweets," Pinkie Pie cries, jumping up and down.

"I hear they sell some marvelous beads and jewelry there, too," Rarity adds. "They will be the perfect finishing touches for my Ponyville uniforms."

"Did you know…" Twilight begins, her head stuck in her travel guide again.

But Rarity and Pinkie Pie have already stopped listening.

"Get yer warm, delicious apple brown Bettys here! It's a Sweet Apple Acres family recipe!" Applejack yells as Rainbow Falls ponies gather around to try this delicacy they've never heard of before.

"But it's not rainbow-colored," one of the Rainbow ponies whispers to her friend, unsure whether to try it.

"It's like a rainbow in your mouth!" the other replies, taking a big bite. "You have to try it!"

Soon, there is a line of Rainbow Falls ponies a mile long, waiting to try Applejack's Bettys!

"I told y'all they'd be a hit here!" Applejack says.

"Shees ahhar dewishwush!" Pinkie Pie says, her mouth exploding with Bettys.

Dear Spike,

Today we spent the day in the Rainbow Falls marketplace. It's a lot like the marketplace in Ponyville, actually. This is where all the Rainbow Falls ponies come to set up their carts and wagons and sell their goods. Ponies were selling rainbow ribbons with medals on them, rainbow glasses, rainbow flags, rainbow horns and megaphones, rainbow foam hooves, rainbow pennants, and unicorn horns—all in honor of the Equestria Games qualifying competition. There were also lots of food carts, and Applejack set up her wagon and sold her apple brown Bettys—which were a huge hit! My first stop tomorrow is the Rainbow Falls arena to watch the Ponyville Flyers practice. Keep up the good work with the animals, and I'll write again soon.

Lots of love,
Twilight

"Okay, Flyers, let's try this one more time!" Rainbow Dash shouts at the top of her lungs.

"Wow, the Rainbow Falls arena is huge!" Twilight Sparkle comments, looking around.

"I know!" Rainbow Dash agrees. "It's the perfect place to practice—now, if Fluttershy and Bulk Biceps could just pass the horseshoe without dropping it, we'd be in business."

"It says in my travel guide that the Rainbow Falls arena was built by the same ponies who built the arena in the Canterlot Castle!" Twilight explains. "And, there are over twenty small tents set up along the sidelines so that each city has its own private area for contestants to wait their turn before competing."

"That's nice, Twilight," Rainbow Dash says, "but if you don't mind, we're trying to concentrate here. The race is only a day away."

"Oh, of course, don't mind me," Twilight replies, stepping away to write a postcard.

Dear Spike,

I spent the day in the Rainbow Falls arena watching everypony practice for the qualifying race. It was so exciting! The arena is enormous, and it's covered from one end to the other in shimmering grass that's the exact same length the whole way across! It says in my book that landscapers groom and measure the grass on the grounds twice a day to make sure it stays in perfect condition. There are all these giant reeds, hoops with horseshoes, arrows, and clouds with rainbows at the top set up all over the arena for the flying relay race. Rainbow Dash and Fluttershy have been practicing so much, I hope they make it! Well, I'm off to go watch them practice some more, but I'll write again to let you know how the qualifying match goes!

Your best friend,
Twilight

That afternoon, the ponies are still at the arena watching practice when one of the Wonderbolts hurts his wings.

"Oh no, it's Soarin!" the Cloudsdale ponies cry out. "Are you okay?"

"I'm hurt," he replies. "I think I need a medic."

"I don't mean to eavesdrop," Twilight cuts in, "but it says here in my travel guide that Rainbow Falls has one of the most advanced hospital facilities in all of Equestria. Maybe we should take him there?"

"That's a great idea!" Pinkie Pie chimes in. "We'll take him for you—we know you probably need to keep practicing."

"Thank you so much," the Cloudsdale ponies reply. "You Ponyville ponies are so friendly and helpful."

"I bet you didn't expect to explore the hospital on your tour of the city," Pinkie Pie says to Twilight as they wait for Soarin to get settled into a bed.

"I can't say that I did," Twilight replies. "But I'm glad we came. My guidebook says that Rainbow Falls Hospital was built with state-of-the-art machines and the latest technological equipment, so I'm sure Soarin is in the best hooves here."

Pinkie Pie and Twilight Sparkle stay until Soarin is all tucked in and feeling better. Then they head back to their hotel to get a good night's sleep. After all, the qualifying competition is tomorrow!

On the day of the competition, the Rainbow Falls arena is full of excitement. Tension is in the air as all the ponies gather on the grounds. The stands up above are full of ponies looking on and cheering for their teams, while the contestants are huddled in their cities' tents, getting ready to compete.

Finally, it's time for the Ponyville Flyers to compete in the relay race competition.

"I'm so nervous, I can hardly breathe," Rarity says to her friends from up in the stands.

"Go, Ponyville, go!" Pinkie Pie cheers, shaking her pom-poms.

"I hope Fluttershy and Bulk Biceps pass the horseshoe without dropping it this time…" Twilight says worriedly.

"So do we!" her friends agree.

Dear Spike,

Ponyville qualified! Fluttershy and Bulk Biceps were great and didn't drop the horseshoe once, and Rainbow Dash was amazing! The second she had that horseshoe in her mouth, she soared through the arena, cruised past the obstacles, and raced onto the winner's platform. I'm so proud of her!

It looks like our trip to Rainbow Falls was a hit. This is a truly great city, but we're all excited to come home! We leave tomorrow. I can't wait to see you and hear about your time with the animals. 'Til then, it's time to go celebrate with the team.

Hugs,

Twilight

"It's great to be home, Spike!" Twilight cries out, giving her number one assistant a hug.

"I sure missed you, Twilight," Spike says. "Thanks for all your postcards. I almost felt like I was there with you."

"Since you couldn't come to Rainbow Falls this time, I decided to bring a little Rainbow Falls to you."

"Thanks, Twilight! You're the best!"

Dear citizens of Ponyville,

As mayor of this great town, it is my honor and privilege to announce that the Ponyville Flyers have qualified to compete in the Equestria Games relay race competition. All the ponies in Ponyville are so very proud of our contestants, and we can't wait to see them shine in the upcoming games in the Crystal Empire. Please join us for a celebration in the town square tomorrow at four o'clock in the afternoon to congratulate our team!

With much pride,
Your Ponyville mayor